This book is dedicated to you, my friend,
and all of the doors that you are destined to walk through.
May you hold the door open so that the next person
who is struggling to get in feels the love, grace, peace, and hope
that only you can bring into the world. —T.M.

To God, who makes all that I do possible. —L.O.

ISBN: 978-1-5460-1256-6

WorthyKids, Hachette Book Group
1290 Avenue of the Americas, New York, NY 10104

Text copyright © 2022 by Tyler Merritt
Art copyright © 2022 by Hachette Book Group, Inc.

Library of Congress Cataloging-in-Publication Data

Names: Merritt, Tyler, author. | Ollivierre, Lonnie, illustrator.
Title: A door made for me / by Tyler Merritt ;
illustrations by Lonnie Ollivierre.
Description: New York, NY : WorthyKids, [2022] | Audience: Ages 5-8. |
Summary: After Tyler's first experience of overt racism, his grandfather
reminds him that another person's hate does not change the fact that he
is loved and perfect just as he is.
Identifiers: LCCN 2021058275 | ISBN 9781546012566 (hardcover)
Subjects: CYAC: Racism—Fiction. | African Americans—Fiction. | LCGFT:
Picture books.
Classification: LCC PZ7.1.M47724 Do 2022 | DDC [E]—dc23
LC record available at https://lccn.loc.gov/2021058275

Designed by Eve DeGrie

Printed and bound in Canada · FRI
2 4 6 8 10 9 7 5 3 1

Written by **TYLER MERRITT**

with *Ty Chapman*

A DOOR MADE FOR ME

Illustrated by Lonnie Ollivierre

WORTHY
kids

I watched our house with its bright blue door get smaller and smaller as we drove away.

I didn't want to spend the summer at my grandparents' house. I didn't know anyone there. **What would I do? Who would I play with?**

Mom said it would all work out, but I didn't believe her until I met Jack.

Jack and I spent our time outside, only heading in to eat and sleep. Mostly, we hunted for nightcrawlers and fished in the river. I had never fished before, and I'd never hunted worms!

I wasn't interested in touching any critter
known for crawling out of the ground at night!
But Jack showed me they weren't so bad.

Usually we only caught a few fish. But one day, we caught three buckets full!

"You're getting really good at this!" Jack beamed.

As the sun started to go down, we scooped up our buckets and headed home.

When we got to our road, Jack walked right by.
"Where are you going?" I asked.
"Do you *see* how many fish we caught? We've got to show everybody! Come on," he said. "It won't take long."
I shrugged and followed along.

We went house to house, knocking on doors and asking if Jack's friends could come out. At the first house, a large man told us Jack's friend couldn't come out as the door quickly closed.

The second house was the same.
We couldn't go in, and no one came out.
Suddenly, my stomach
was doing flips.

What's going on? I wondered.
Why won't Jack's friends come outside?

We figured we'd try one last time.

We walked up to a house with a beautiful wooden door.
I knocked and we waited patiently, until, *creeeak*, the
door swung open slowly.
A woman towered above us, frowning. ***Another adult***,
I thought. ***And she doesn't look happy.***

Jack asked if his friend could come out. The woman shook her head and pointed at Jack.

"You can come in, Jack" she said. "But not that little Black boy. He needs to stay outside."

I felt all the air leave my body as Jack walked inside to show off the fish we had caught together. "I'll be right back," he promised.

The door shut tight behind Jack, followed by the loudest lock I had ever heard.

I turned and left my share of
fish baking in the sinking sun.

I couldn't stop thinking about the slam of
the door and the click of the lock.

I had already walked through lots of doors.
The glass double doors of my school, the
bright blue one at my house, and the impossibly
heavy one at my grandparents' place.

I didn't understand. **Why had this door
slammed shut at the sight of me?**

When I walked into the
house, I sat down on the floor.

Grandpa sat beside me.
"What's wrong?" he said.
I told him the whole story.
He shook his head. "I wish
this didn't still happen,
especially not to you, Tyler."
"But why did it?" I asked.
"How can she hate me when
she doesn't know me?"

Grandpa sighed. **"I wish I knew.**

"In life," he said, "there are many doors, but some people don't want to see us walk through them.
"It can be for any reason: the way you're dressed, the twists and curls of your glorious hair, or even the beautiful mahogany of your skin.

"It won't make sense. You might feel angry or sad, and that's okay.

**"But remember, sweet boy,
you are loved.
And you are perfect
just as you are.**

"Another person's hate doesn't change that. You'll find a door that's right for you— and when you do, be sure to leave it open for the next kid struggling to get in."

I kept on catching fish that summer, and Grandpa taught me how to clean them and fry them up. I was still sad about the woman who slammed her door in my face, and I missed playing with Jack.

He came by once to see if I wanted to catch nightcrawlers together. I told him no. I didn't hate Jack, but it was hard to stay friends after what he did.

Grandpa told me not to give up on Jack. He said, "I know it hurts. But he's still learning. I think he'll be a better friend someday."

I hoped he was right.

Not a lot of doors opened for me that summer.
It wasn't right, and it wasn't fair. But I knew there
were more doors waiting just around the corner.

I would find a door for me.

I'd open it myself—
and hold it wide for
whoever wanted to come in.

A Note from the Author

The story you just read about young Tyler is *my* story.

I've always loved my rich, dark skin. I remember looking in the mirror as a child and being amazed by how my eyes looked like the color of coffee. I loved that I could pat my short afro into a perfectly round circle. Growing up in Las Vegas, I was surrounded by people who looked different than me. It was normal, expected. So it wasn't until that door shut in my face on a summer day that I realized my beautiful mahogany skin would be a problem for some people.

That moment left a mark on my heart that I would carry for many years. I'm so thankful I had loved ones around to remind me how special I was. They steered me in the direction of love and forgiveness and understanding. And I want you to know that you, my friend, are special too.

And what about Jack? When his friend Tyler was turned away because of how he looked, Jack left him standing outside. How would you react in that situation? Are there things you could do or say to support your friend? To help your friend feel less alone? Are there ways you can hold a door open for those who might not always be invited in?

Jack's reaction was hurtful to Tyler, but there is always grace for the missteps that we make. My friend Jack was able to learn that our mistakes are patiently waiting for us to turn them into lessons. He became the better friend I so deeply hoped he would.

As you read this story, I invite you to walk with me through a moment of hardship that taught me a lifelong lesson: *You are precisely who you are meant to be.* Your specific brand of awesomeness will lead you through so many doors made just for you. I can't wait to meet you on the other side.

Cheering you on,
Tyler Merritt